For Catherine and Melissa
and all the animals at Rising Moon Farm
P. R.

For Janice
S. G.

First published 2004 by Walker Books Ltd
87 Vauxhall Walk, London SE11 5HJ

2 4 6 8 10 9 7 5 3 1

Text © 2004 Phyllis Root

Illustrations © 2004 Susan Gaber

This book has been typeset in Cochin

Printed in China

British Library Cataloguing in Publication Data:
a catalogue record for this book is available
from the British Library

ISBN 0-7445-8541-4

www.walkerbooks.co.uk

Ten Sleepy Sheep

Phyllis Root illustrated by Susan Gaber

WALKER BOOKS
AND SUBSIDIARIES
LONDON · BOSTON · SYDNEY · AUCKLAND

"Time to sleep,"
call the mother sheep
in the grass knee-deep.
But ten little sheep
don't want to sleep.

10

Ten little sheep

leap the cucumber vine.

Long grass bends.

Spider mends.

Sleep, sheep.

Now there are …

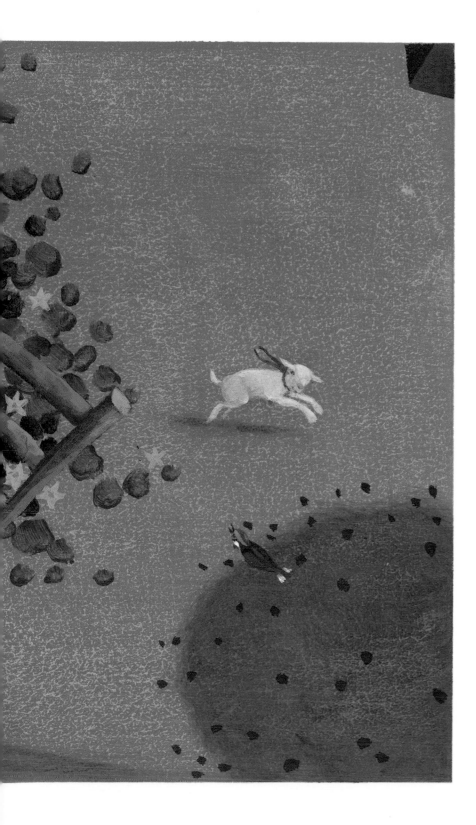

9

Nine sheep race
past the tall green gate.

Wind sighs.

Whip-poor-will cries.

Sleep, sheep.

Now there are ...

8

Eight sheep romp
by the rose of heaven.

Blossoms close.

Ducklings doze.

Sleep, sheep.

Now there are …

7

Seven sheep crash

through a stack of sticks.

Mouse explores.

Old dog snores.

Sleep, sheep.

Now there are …

6

Six sheep roam
by the old beehive.
Bees hum.
Crickets thrum.
Sleep, sheep.

Now there are …

5

Five sheep scoot
past the red-barn door.
Swallows swoop.
Barn owls whoop.
Sleep, sheep.

Now there are ...

4

Four sheep amble
by the apple tree.
Fireflies blink.
First stars wink.

Sleep, sheep.

Now there are …

3

Three sheep splash
past the blue canoe.
Tall reeds swish.
Herons fish.
Sleep, sheep.

Now there are …

2

Two sheep lope
by the rabbit run.

Kitten stirs.

Grey cat purrs.

Sleep, sheep.

Now there is …

1

One sheep bleats,

"Mama, I can't sleep."

"Hush," says her mother.

"Have you tried counting sheep?"

One by the vine,

one by the gate,

one by the rose,

one by the sticks,

one by the hive,

one by the door,

one by the tree,

one by the canoe,

one by the rabbit run …

and one little sheep
in the grass knee-deep,
nestled by her mother,
fast asleep.